To Alfie.

Best wishes

M J Stanley

Kids in Shorts

MELODY STARKEY

Matador
9 Priory Business Park,
Wistow Road, Kibworth Beauchamp,
Leicestershire. LE8 0RX
Tel: 0116 279 2299
Email: books@troubador.co.uk
Web: www.troubador.co.uk/matador
Twitter: @matadorbooks

ISBN 978 1788034 685

British Library Cataloguing in Publication Data.
A catalogue record for this book is available from the British Library.

Printed and bound in the UK by TJ International, Padstow, Cornwall
Typeset in 11pt Garamond by Troubador Publishing Ltd, Leicester, UK

Matador is an imprint of Troubador Publishing Ltd

Thanks must firstly go to Charlee Carter from Wyken Croft Primary School, who suggested the title for this new collection.

This book is dedicated to the intriguing characters I have been fortunate enough to meet, many of whom have been the inspiration for these stories.

It is also written to pay tribute to all those children who manage to live their lives successfully despite their problems and difficult situations.

Contents

All Change

The whole family were running for the train. Euston was as busy as ever and Laura was the slowest; exhausted from an exciting day in the capital, her legs seemed to turn to jelly as she struggled up the steps to the platform. Her twin brothers raced ahead, taking two at a time, Mum and Dad leading the way, both used to running as a means of keeping fit. So Laura puffed and panted, and to her horror, lost sight of everyone in the throngs of people around her.

Eventually, she struggled to the top of the same steps, but didn't know whether to turn left or right.

Which platform? she thought wildly, looking anxiously all about her. In a panic, she ran to the left, changed her mind and went back to the right. She ran, her heart now thumping in her chest with the effort, straining to see over the wall at the top, and eventually she ran down the steps to find herself on the platform. Was this the train? No idea!

A long express stood on Platform 5. None of the steely grey doors were open, no one hanging out of the windows looking for her or calling her name. None of her family to be seen ANYWHERE.

They must be on here! she convinced herself and pressed the circular button which thankfully lit up its green light, and the heavy door slid open. She jumped on board, clutching her badge-covered rucksack in front of her, always frightened it would slip down onto the rails if she didn't. Immediately after, the whistle was heard, and the train started to pull away.

Luckily, the announcement reassured her that she at least was on the right train:

"… stopping at Coventry…" That's all she wanted to hear. She sank down into the huge plush seat. Where were they? After a while she got her breath back and paced up and down several carriages. Most people had settled down to sleep or had headphones plugged in. She felt utterly alone and quite tearful.

At ten years old, Laura was very sensible and not given to panicking; but this was really scary. Maybe her family would call her. She knew she had no credit left on her phone – but there weren't even any missed calls.

They will be waiting for me at the other end, she told herself firmly, but she wasn't convinced.

It seemed a long journey from London. Laura sipped her lukewarm bottle of water. Her tummy rumbled. No money to buy tea. She tried hard not to let anyone see the tears that were starting to fall down her cheeks. She turned her head towards the window, alarmed to see how quickly it had become almost completely dark.

Eventually, after what seemed like an eternity, the information panel showed her:

The next station will be Coventry.

She looked up to double-check. Coventry. Yes. Standing by the door, she couldn't quite make out the station signs. As soon as the green light lit up the door button, she pressed it and jumped out. The heavy door slid shut behind her.

Funny, she thought to herself, *this must be a different end to the platform; it looks strange.*

The train slid off into thick darkness, its red tail-lights blinking dimly as it went. Then to her utter dismay, she realised that the announcement had been wrong! This was Rugby! Miles away. How could she have been so stupid? Why didn't she check the signs? No wonder she didn't recognise the platform! It was deserted. Sunday night, nine o'clock, not even a station official in sight.

Then, mercifully, a figure appeared around the corner of the station café, shut now, of course. It was a tall lady with extraordinarily long blonde hair, wearing a floor-length royal blue cape. She looked straight at Laura as she drew nearer.

"Are you lost?"

Laura hesitated, always told not to speak to strangers – but what choice did she have? And, after all, she looked kind. Laura explained how she had got off the train by mistake, thinking it was Coventry, and was waiting for her parents to call.

"I'm going to Coventry," the lady said simply, lowering her head so that Laura could see her brilliant blue eyes, even in the poor light. "Don't worry," the lady reassured her. "I'm a teacher, well, helper if you like, and Coventry is my home; there's another train in a few minutes, so everything will be all right."

The lady talked gently about how she liked helping poor people in the city and altering how they were treated. She produced a small cloth bag of bright red apples and Laura gratefully munched on one when it was offered.

The train came as the lady had predicted and they both

got on. Laura was relieved to be surrounded by other people. The lady wasn't scary, but there was something about her...

In no time at all it was clear they were approaching Coventry, its unmistakeable three spires silhouetted against the yellowy pink lights produced by the city's neon glow. They got off together and there standing with anxious faces – Mum, Dad and the twins. Laura ran towards them, crying openly now.

Many hugs later, she turned to introduce the lady who had acted so kindly towards her – but she had already walked towards the exit, her cloak drawn tightly against her, long golden tresses blowing in the soft breeze. Then she just seemed to vanish.

When Laura told her family about her, the twins joked about imagining things – but they were really all just glad she was back with them safe and sound.

The incident was often talked about, but never really resolved. Many weeks later, on a rainy day in the half-term holidays, Laura was in the local art gallery and museum. As she passed the section that talked about Lady Godiva and her work in the city all those years ago, Laura couldn't help but be fascinated by the various paintings of this famous woman – in particular, her brilliant blue eyes...

An Unexpected Ally

The morning sun rose lazily above the terracotta tiled roof opposite Flora's bedroom window, and George, her playful black Labrador, stirred at the foot of her dishevelled bed. All of a sudden she was wide awake and realised with some trepidation that it was Sunday. Not any run-of-the-mill Sunday, full of homework, bike rides and church. Church! That was it! Today was the day when she was to lead part of the service. That sounded easy enough, but to stand there with scores of unblinking faces looking at her expectedly...

"You can do it!" Dad assured her cheerily, chivvying her younger brother Robert, who had been sent back to the bathroom to wash *behind* his ears. "No problem, it's only fifteen minutes!"

Yes, fifteen minutes to trip up over your words, hiccup or worse still, FREEZE and not remember what you wanted to say. Then they would all laugh and nudge each other, especially Derek Price, a boy in her church group who teased her constantly at every opportunity about absolutely everything.

Flora sighed a little and pushed away the excited George who expected an early morning ball game.

"Not today," Flora muttered to herself a little sulkily. "I've got to PREPARE, George. STOP it!" Her young pet rolled over and tried to look appealing.

Ignoring him, the young schoolgirl, newly in Year 7, quickly showered and dressed.

Mum was all smiles, trying hard not to make a big deal out of the occasion.

"Please don't tell me *you'll be all right!*" whispered Flora, smoothing her silky strawberry blonde hair into a neat ponytail.

"Would I?" smiled Mum, hugging her, proud already.

"I won't make faces!" promised Robert.

"Too right you won't!" said Dad firmly, leading him to the breakfast table.

*

The journey to church was much too short and in no time at all their dusty estate car drew up outside the church steps.

"You go ahead and get set up!" called Mum from the driving seat. "I know, I know; I won't say it!" She reached over and smoothed a wisp of hair away from Flora's piercing blue eyes. "Show me that lovely smile!"

Robert gave her an exaggerated 'thumbs up' sign and went off with Dad to save some front row seats. *Not the FRONT row,* Flora thought; a sudden flash of panic across her crowded young mind.

Flora just about took control of a very wobbly bottom lip and gathered her tapestry bag full of 'props'. Derek Price appeared annoyingly at the corner of the car park, grinning stupidly at her. So Flora ran as quickly as she could up the steps. Then it happened.

Without warning, she found herself spreadeagled on the church steps, her papers, pens and pictures scattered

everywhere. She could think of nothing but the agonising pain in her right knee.

"Whoops!" smirked Derek and he was about to make another snide comment when he caught sight of the acute pain spreading across her freckled face.

He ran off, intent at first on showing that the incident was nothing to do with him; but then with a change of heart, he ran over to Flora's mum who was just coming through the car park gate.

"Mrs Morris! Come quickly, it's Flora…"

Eleanor Morris eyed the youth suspiciously, but realised that he wasn't joking, by the real urgency in his usually whiney voice.

They both ran back to the steps. By now a small crowd had gathered around Flora, who was a deathly white, tears streaming down her cheeks.

Dad and Robert running over.

Mum trying to stay calm.

Mr Weeks the local paramedic, a reassuring presence; someone had dialled 999.

Flora slipped in and out of consciousness, as Mr Weeks' strong, trained hands lifted her gingerly onto the stretcher.

"Straight to hospital," he grinned reassuringly. "Nothing to worry about…"

Well, there is, Flora thought dimly, then nothing registered until she was lying in the strangely high, cold hospital bed.

NOTHING was going right – even when they got home. After a week of blurred experiences in the children's ward, Flora almost expected to be able to be walking again when she reached the comfort of her own home. They'd only moved in about a week before, but it was the kind of place which had a warm, welcoming atmosphere as though it had been loved and cared for in the past. How she had longed to be there. But in cold reality, she couldn't walk – her right leg plastered from hip to ankle with a fiddly thing in the middle which had to be altered every few days. She couldn't go outside on her own; she couldn't get a drink or a snack, let alone go to the bathroom! School was out of the question for a week at least. There was one bright spot in the day when friends would pop in on their way home, bringing gigantic boxes of chocolates and sticky home-made get well cards.

But apart from that, it was so BORING! As the days passed, she began to worry. What if she couldn't walk properly again – ever? She pushed this frightening thought to the very back of her mind like a piece of unattempted homework in a dark drawer.

The day that Derek Price knocked on the door at four o'clock had been spent in tears. The physio had said things would improve, but she had to try. TRY?! How could she when it hurt so much? She'd been back to school for a few hours, but everything was such an effort. Everyone was almost unbearably kind. Flora's normally sunny nature had been choked, it seemed, by the STRUGGLE of just managing everything.

Derek Price was the last person she wanted to see, but one miserable Monday, after school, he knocked at the door. Both parents insisted on politeness at all times, and he was ushered rather sheepishly into the cosy front room where she lay on the new chocolate brown corner sofa, her temporary bed.

"All right then?" he asked, rather embarrassed now,

shoving a rather grimy bag of slightly withered grapes towards her.

"Er… thanks," she muttered, embarrassed too.

Robert put his head round the door.

"Ooh, sorry!" he giggled, only to be hoiked out of the way by Dad who was on his way to his night shift.

"Perhaps Derek can help you with those exercises!" he winked at her.

*

It became a bit of a routine. Derek came every other day, and rather than the annoying pest he had seemed to be at church, he turned out to be, well, okay really. He pretended to be injured too and Mum was pleased to hear the laughter that ensued as he became too enthusiastic and fell over.

Little by little, Flora's strength and good mood returned. The day the plaster came off, Derek was there, hanging about by the gate as she hobbled up the path with the help of her new crutches.

"You won't need me to come round any more!" he said, a hint of real sadness in his voice.

"Oh yes I will, Derek Price," retorted Flora brightly. "You don't get off that easily; you're helping me do that presentation next week!"

Fire and Ice

The plane landed smoothly on the tarmac, not a snowflake in sight. Well, it was July, but you would expect Iceland to be cold at least.

Stuart tidied his pull-down tray and slotted his things into the handy compartments of his special bag. The lovely teaching assistant who had helped him so much in primary school had given it to him as a leaving present, knowing that Stuart would love its internal organisation.

He felt happier now, everything in order. The journey had been stressful; all those noisy passengers, tipping litter into the narrow gangway and down the sides of the tight seats. Stuart knew he worried because he was special. "On the spectrum," they said at school – very bright, though – bright smiles at least from the Special Needs Co-ordinator; but Stuart thought he saw a worried look in her eyes. Fortunately, his mum wasn't worried – just wanted life to be easier for him.

Everything was fine at home: tidy bedroom, shoes lined up exactly, timetable on the wall; even the cat knew she had to stay on her cushion. But everywhere else could be a struggle, like when the taxi had been early this morning and Stuart had refused to get in until it was the right time...

*

Family friends picked them up from the airport in a battered white minibus and Stuart spent the journey to the other side of Reykjavik with his nose pressed to the window, hugging his special bag, a little nervous by now. Where would he sleep? Where was the bathroom? How would he get on because he knew it wouldn't get very dark? Good job he'd packed his Batman mask!

"Come on, Stuart, time to get out," Mum said gently.

Dad was working in the city that summer and so the whole family had been invited to stay with his parents' friends. Inga was Icelandic and her husband Alan spoke the language, as he had worked there for many years.

The stunning house where they were staying, with its bleached beams and wide open rooms, was really welcoming. The family who lived there knew Stuart well; so he felt at ease after a few doubtful moments when he first walked through the beautifully carved wooden front door.

It was a bit strange putting on his swimming shorts in the rain and sitting in the hot tub out on the enormous patio, but Alan sat beside him and chatted about the plans for the holiday and Stuart committed them to memory, down to the very last detail.

They had a wonderful first few days. Everything really well organised – gorgeous waterfalls that you could actually walk behind, exciting geysers that shot out of the rocky ground unexpectedly. Even Stuart laughed at that – but the smell of sulphur was horrendous! He was even persuaded to eat pickled shark out of a musty jar!

One of the absolute best days was at the Blue Lagoon,

where Mum persuaded him to plaster his face with white mud – well, most people were doing it. Had to make sure there was the same amount on both sides, though!

He didn't feel so good on the whale-watching trip. Even the commonly seen minke whales were elusive. It was a dull, grey day with a dull, grey sea and his stomach felt even greyer. So Stuart was glad to get back to the hot tub. He'd got used to it by now as he had going to bed in the daylight; with his mask pulled firmly down over his eyes, he managed to sleep soundly, worn out by his adventures.

Inga had persuaded them to book a trip to the glacier one particularly rainy day. They were met by an exciting 4 by 4 with the word *Thundercloud* emblazoned on it in shiny blue. She was full of excitement as always. Stuart marvelled at her fearlessness. Mum seemed quite timid in comparison.

It was an ordeal putting on their dark blue snowsuits which were compulsory for every traveller. Well, they'd been worn by other people, so they were dusty and smelt funny. However, only Stuart seemed to notice this. Alan, calm as always, just zipped him up and reassured him that everything would be okay.

When they finally reached the top of the glacier, the sun made the snow sparkle like a Christmas cake. The weather at the top was absolutely gorgeous: freezing but beautiful and they could look right down to see the toy-like city below, swathed in cloud and rain. The family from Chile who had shared the 4 by 4 (and, bizarrely, sang Beatles songs throughout the whole journey) were now racing about throwing snowballs at each other as it was such a novelty for them.

"Do you want to go on a snowmobile or a dog sled?" asked Alan, his face breaking into a broad grin as Stuart hadn't known about this treat. He was clearly so excited.

"Oh, a snowmobile, please, Uncle Alan." His answer was a mere whisper.

Alan and Stuart made their way to the row of gleaming machines and were issued with strict instructions on how to avoid sinkholes which could be extremely dangerous.

Stuart listened intently, mentally noting every detail, and he studied the map closely. Alan was his confident self, assuring him that he knew where to go anyway. Mum and Inga went off on a dog sled in a flurry of snow, amid much barking and yelping. The hugely excitable animals didn't appeal to Stuart – too unpredictable!

"Don't touch them before we feed them!" the driver had warned. That was enough to put Stuart off.

Alan was an experienced rider; he was good at most things and Stuart sat behind him with his oversized crash helmet jammed firmly over his eyes, clinging to Alan's waist like a limpet.

"Right, here we go. Hold on tight!"

They set off slowly – the conditions were superb; the sun cast sharp shadows across the perfect snow. The way was marked by tall coloured poles, to guide travellers away from dangerous areas of melted ice. Alan sped expertly round them, chatting as he went.

Stuart was thrilled and felt safe in his expert hands, that was until suddenly the poles vanished and Alan quickly slowed the throbbing machine right down.

"Oh dear, it looks like we'll have to turn back," he squinted into the distance, "it's not safe without the poles."

So, much to Stuart's dismay, Alan turned round and they made their way steadily back towards the base.

It was Stuart who heard it first.

"Stop!" he shouted above the noise of the engine. Alan, used to Stuart's worries, obligingly came to a halt.

"Did you hear that?" Stuart pointed in a westerly direction towards the setting sun.

"Sorry, mate, couldn't hear much above the engine."

Stuart took off his helmet and there it was: a loud cry – a bird maybe – or what? It came from the point at which the poles stopped.

Alan shook his head and also removed his helmet.

There it was again, louder this time and more like a human sound – yes, the unmistakeable cry of:

"Help!"

Alan and Stuart looked at each other and then Alan got out his phone – but there was no signal here.

"Help! Please help – anybody!" Then again, in Icelandic: "Hjalp!"

"Someone's in trouble," Alan looked concerned, frowning into his useless phone.

"But I know the way," Stuart, matter-of-fact as always – it was obvious to him. He had a near-photographic memory and had memorised every marker on the map that they had been shown earlier.

There was little choice really – they were a good thirty minutes from the base and in that time what might happen to a person in trouble up here?

"Alan, it's fine – I know the way to go!" Stuart insisted.

Could he trust the young lad's judgement?

"Alan, please!" Stuart was agitated and shaking.

"Right, we'll just go carefully…"

Alan restarted the snowmobile. When they got to the last pole, there was still no one in sight, but the cries continued, louder than ever.

"Turn right by that rock," Stuart was definite and clear in his instruction. "Now straight on for 400 metres, then left where there is a slight hill."

Images of them both vanishing down a large sinkhole flashed through Alan's mind – after all, he was the responsible adult here…

"Right now, keep going straight…"

Then they saw an overturned snowmobile – but no sign of its rider.

"Here, quickly…"

Alan got off and carefully made his way to where it was lying. Stuart sat still, holding his breath.

"Stuart, quickly, there's a length of rope in the emergency pack. Throw it over to me!"

Alan seemed to be peering down a large hole. Stuart pulled out the thick yellow rope with trembling hands and managed to slide it across the ice.

"There's someone down here!" he shouted above the wind which had suddenly got up. "Whatever you do, stay on the seat; it's too dangerous!"

Alan was a strong man and eventually he seemed to be heaving a small bedraggled figure out of what would have been icy water. She was so lucky; moments later and the dreadful cold would have got the better of her.

Somehow the three of them managed to get back to base, Stuart directing them for the first blank kilometre. The young woman, for that's who it was, sandwiched between them both.

*

"What I don't understand," remarked the head ranger much later, after the rescue helicopter had taken the rescued lady to the nearest hospital, "is how you knew where to go without the markers. They'd obviously been swept away in the storm we had last week."

Alan smiled and gestured to Stuart.

"This is a very special young man. He's going to be so useful in years to come – a real benefit to society!"

Mum hugged her son, still in his huge ill-fitting snowsuit.

"Oh, I know that already!" she smiled.

"You need to put your poles back," Stuart said matter-of-factly, and adjusted the maps on the counter so they were all in order.

Guy Fawkes

Bonfire Night was always special, making a deliciously exciting event at the start of such a dull, depressing month.

However, the weather this year had been glorious right to the end of October and beyond. For days the sun had been shining, making the gorgeous colours of the autumn trees sharp: vivid and brilliant against an almost crisply azure sky.

Now on November 5th, blissfully a Saturday, the whole village seemed to be out, dragging various pieces of wood from their cars and hoisting them onto the ever-growing bonfire in the middle of the football field.

Jenny's mum was on the committee, organising such events in the village, and so the whole family became involved. Not that Jenny minded much; and when she saw her friend Pilar across the road, she intended to include her in the preparations too.

Pilar was always fun. She had a Spanish mum and an English dad; they had settled here when both parents started new jobs in England. Pilar had been born in Madrid, but her English was improving daily, yet her mistakes were always good for a laugh. She wouldn't realise when she had said something odd, but was warmly good-humoured and would widen her big brown eyes with mock annoyance when people corrected her.

Jenny in turn was trying to learn Spanish.

"¡Muy bien, mi amiga!" Pilar would say and then talk really quickly, rolling her 'r's in an exaggerated way to confuse her English friend even more.

"I no understand," Pilar commented as they dragged a particularly splintery piece of wood all the way across the dewy grass, "why we build this fire!"

"Well, it's to burn Guy Fawkes on!" grinned Jenny, stamping on the wood to break it up.

"Who is this Guy Fawkes?" Pilar screwed up her nose as she always did when she couldn't quite understand an idea or a word.

"Well, he called himself Guido when he fought for the Spanish." Jenny was always good at historical facts.

"He was Español then?"

"Oh no, he was English, born in York. He tried to make friends with the Spanish because he wanted to try to change the English religion to Catholicism. He wanted to blow up everyone in the Houses of Parliament, including the Protestant king."

"He was a bad man, then, this Guido; he didn't deserve Spanish friends!" Pilar was curious, "Is this why you burn him?"

"I suppose people wanted to show he was a bad man by burning a model of him."

Pilar shuddered.

"I don't like this English costume!"

"Custom!" Jenny giggled. "Hey, there's an idea, we could make one!"

"¿Que? How do we do this?"

"Oh, just get some old clothes, stuff them with newspaper and draw a mask. Yes! Venga!"

Pilar, still confused, but caught up in her friend's enthusiasm, asked her parents if she could go to Jenny's house, and they spent the entire afternoon making a giant Guy Fawkes.

The cat didn't like it at all, and ran off tail down when he saw it.

Well, it did look odd. Dad's old trousers, stuffed unevenly with all manner of newspapers and magazines so that they created an almost alien-like effect. Jenny's faded school shirt was filled so tightly it appeared to have massive biceps. Pilar, a talented artist, sketched out a grotesque mask. They looked at pictures on the internet and she copied his 'goatie' beard.

Towards five o'clock, the light was fading; a gorgeous orange glow filtered into Jenny's room and the effigy stood as if looking at the bonfire across the field.

"¡Está asustado!" muttered Pilar. "He is frightened, and I no like it!"

"Oh, Pilar; it's only fun!" Jenny drew a big crimson grin on the mask with exaggerated teeth. The sombre mood broken, they hoisted their awkward creation down the stairs and stood him up in the hallway. The cat shot past, his yellow eyes wide with fright.

"It does look slightly scary," grinned Mum. "Right, let's get him onto the bonfire, while it's safe."

Lots of people commented on their 'new friend' and he was given pride of place high up right at the front of the fire.

"It seems a shame to burn him," sighed Jenny.

Pilar went home to get some warmer clothes and then made her way back to Jenny's on her own, her parents stopping to buy sparklers from the village shop. Pilar ran the last few metres along the path towards Jenny's house, really excited about the evening ahead.

By now all the street lamps were lit, but the sky was still a beautiful mixture of burnt orange and deep scarlet, the village church silhouetted like a cut-out black shape. Pilar stopped, always keen to appreciate natural beauty; then she turned and looked at the huge bonfire. What she saw next made her turn cold.

The precariously balanced Guy Fawkes figure certainly looked real in this light and, more disturbingly, his left arm appeared to be — well, waving side to side, then both arms, as Pilar drew nearer.

Really frightened by now, she ran to Jenny's front door and banged on it with her fists. It was opened by Jenny's dad, a little taken aback.

"Hey, Pilar, what's the matter? ¡Qué pasa?" He knew a few basic Spanish phrases.

She replied in Spanish, flustered, yet eager to explain.

"Hey, slow down. ¡No comprendo!" He held her shaking shoulders while she explained in faltering English what she had seen.

Jenny's dad, suspecting the teenagers in the village were up to no good, led the frightened girl up to the field where Jenny and her mum were helping to sort out the hot dogs.

"Pilar's worried about Guy Fawkes," said Dad softly. "We think someone is playing a trick."

Pilar wasn't convinced.

"No trick," she muttered. "I see what I see!"

She explained to Jenny, who, wide-eyed, clutched her friend's arm.

"Let's tell Mr Kenyon. He'll know what to do," gulped Jenny.

"I'm sure it's just kids…" began Dad, but Jenny was off, seeking out Mr Kenyon, a retired policeman now, but always reliable. He'd sort it out — she hoped.

Three large men from the committee, in fluorescent yellow jackets, crossed the safety perimeter fence and made their way towards the bonfire. Guy Fawkes could just be seen, but didn't appear to be moving at all. Pilar stood absolutely still, glued to the scene.

"He moves, I tell you. He moves!"

Then everything seemed to happen at once; a shout from one of the men and then another ran back to the fence.

"Ambulance, quickly!" he shouted to Mr Kenyon.

Minutes later, blue lights were flashing into the field.

*

It turned out that two casual workers, hired for fruit and vegetable picking by a local farmer, had been sheltering or resting next to the bonfire and both had fallen asleep. No one had seen them in the dark. Mercifully, although a bit shaken and certainly surprised, they didn't need to be taken to hospital.

The bonfire wasn't lit; it had to be demolished, just to be sure no one else had crept inside.

"How come that lovely young Spanish girl said the Guy Fawkes was moving?" asked Mr Kenyon afterwards, scratching his head under his homemade pom-pom hat. "Good job she saw something, though. I dread to think what might have happened!"

"Guido Fawkes wasn't such a bad man after all then!" commented Pilar with a smile the day after.

The effigy smiled back. It seemed a shame to burn him now.

Music Lessons

"I really don't see the point!" groaned Charlie, slamming his music books across the table and dragging his fingers haphazardly along the shiny ivory keys of the piano.

"We had this agreement," Mum spoke quietly but firmly, "out of all the things you do, this has cost the most, what with the new piano and all the exams. Now you've got this far, you will carry on until grade 8 and then you'll always be able to play."

"But Sam Frost began and gave it up!" Charlie glowered at his reflection in the glossy panel of the beautiful instrument.

"Yes, but Sam Frost had only been playing for three weeks and didn't have a new piano bought for him!"

Mum looked at the dilapidated kitchen units – new ones sacrificed for the sake of a better piano...

"Well, Dad wouldn't..." Charlie began and then realised he was on dodgy ground. Mum and Dad didn't live together any more but were careful to abide by the same rules; and although Dad didn't pretend to be as enthusiastic about music as he was about sport, he always supported Mum's decisions about what he should or should not do.

"Okay, but just until six o'clock!" mumbled Charlie.

"Deal!" Mum grinned, turning back to simultaneously

cooking the dinner and checking her emails. "Have you done your scales?"

Charlie sighed, and soon the kitchen was filled with the almost soothing sound of arpeggios played over and over.

Half an hour later, as they were eating spaghetti, Mum and Charlie discussed plans for the weekend.

"I've got cross-country on Saturday morning and the swimming gala in the evening." Charlie's eyes lit up. "Are you coming too?"

"Of course!"

Mum and Dad put their differences aside to support him in all his interests.

Scale practice done and excused the washing up if he would play some more, the kitchen echoed with the pleasant sound of songs from *Les Misérables*. Charlie loved this musical and enjoyed being able to play simple versions of the tunes. He would never admit it to his parents, but the music was very comforting to him in times when he felt a little insecure, and he secretly enjoyed being able to make sense of the notes in front of him.

Not that he mentioned it to his friends at school, apart from his best friend George Cresswell, to whom he moaned about the necessity of practice. He talked to them about running, swimming and the latest computer games – which he *wasn't* going to get for Christmas; Mum and Dad didn't approve.

"Can't you buy them yourself?" George suggested in the playground the next morning. He lived in a massive house and money never seemed to be a problem.

"Oh, I'm not really bothered." Charlie dismissed the topic – and partly this was true, he just talked about the games because everyone else did.

George then proceeded to ramble on about his extensive collection and Charlie pretended to be listening; but thankfully a football landed at his feet and a group kickabout began in the precious ten minutes before the bell for start of school.

Assembly was as boring as ever. Charlie and George weren't allowed to sit together in case they chatted, but nevertheless, managed to exchange sidelong silly faces along the line when Mrs Johnson wasn't looking. The usual notices were read out by the phase leader, Mrs Wiffen, who enthused in her usual extravagant style about the carol concert for the local elderly residents.

"And if anyone would like to help with the organisation, please see me at playtime in my room. I'm sure you'd like to help, Charlie Walters!" She had caught the silly face procedure. She never missed any slight misdemeanour; brilliant blue eyes boring into him, so that he turned a bright puce colour.

"It might be okay, you know!" George muttered through a mouthful of apple on their way out at playtime, "if it's in the morning, we'll miss maths!"

So the two friends giggled and swaggered into Mrs Wiffen's room, realising they were the only boys to volunteer. She issued them all with her characteristically neatly typed programme details.

"You will be serving our guests with teas and mince pies and TALKING to them. I expect you'll be good at that, George. Nice to see you offering to help," she added. "Not that I've forgotten it's maths at that time!" She smiled at them both, secretly liking the two troublemakers.

"Honest naughty lads!" she confided with her colleagues, who probably didn't share her sentiments.

*

The day of the concert arrived and much to Charlie and George's delight, they had to miss literacy too. Their classmates looked on enviously as they got out their grammar books.

"Enjoy your lesson, folks!" Charlie elbowed his friend, "Come on, George. You have to get your waiter's outfit on!"

Mrs Wiffen insisted that they wore smart trousers and a tie, inspecting their hands and sending them to scrub their grimy fingernails before it was due to start.

In fairness, Charlie and George did a really good job; it had to be said, more with the talking aspect than the serving of refreshments. Then the choir were led in by Mrs Wiffen, all fiddling with their tinsel decorations and looking slightly embarrassed. They lined up on the stage, Mrs Wiffen glowering at them so that they remained silent. The first readings began and the first carol was introduced. Mrs Johnson started the CD player for the first backing track. But not a sound came out of the ancient dusty machine at the back of the hall. One or two choir members smirked. Mrs Wiffen tutted to herself. Ten minutes later and still no music. Three CD players later and it was obviously a problem with the electrics. The caretaker was called, but was off duty and nowhere to be found. By now, the senior citizens were quite happily chatting amongst themselves and the choir followed suit.

Mrs Wiffen was beside herself. *Why hadn't she checked the music system?* she thought to herself crossly. She glanced nervously at the hall door, hoping the headteacher wouldn't surface from his office just yet.

"Oh dear!" Mrs Wiffen pretended to be calm. "Does anyone play the piano?"

No one volunteered.

Charlie looked down at his shoes and then surreptitiously at the simple music in the spare hymn book open on the radiator.

"You'll always be able to play…" Mum's words echoed in his head.

"Mrs Wiffen, Charlie plays the piano!" George's loud voice interrupted the hum of conversation and everyone turned towards him.

"Well, Charlie, I didn't know that!"

And before he could protest he found himself being firmly steered towards the ancient instrument at the front of the hall.

"But…!" His faint protestations were ignored by Mrs Wiffen, who flicked through the hymn book to 'O Little Town of Bethlehem' and smiled at him brightly.

"Charlie just needs a few minutes to practise!" she reassured the crowded hall.

Using the soft pedal, he followed the notes surprisingly easily to produce the melody with his right hand and gradually added the left for the simple chords.

"There, perfect! Just play it over and over until I signal you to stop!" Mrs Wiffen stood at the front of the choir and the concert began.

It was difficult at first, and his fingers slipped to produce a couple of wrong notes, but no one seemed to notice. Thankfully, the hymn book contained very easy versions of all the carol music and, as he played, he realised what a thrill it gave him to perform in front of others: almost as good as winning a cross-country race!

George's large brown eyes widened behind his tortoiseshell glasses. Was this really his wayward friend he was watching?

The applause at the end was indeed more for the pianist than for the singers. Mrs Wiffen beamed at him.

"Well, Charlie Waters, who would have thought it! Headteacher's award next week for saving the day!"

Mum, of course, was so proud when he told her that evening; but more importantly for Charlie, his friends were really impressed, comparing him to their favourite pop band members.

Somehow music lessons now didn't seem such a waste of time...

Pirate

The sea that day was rough and unwelcoming. Spiteful, sudden waves exploded onto the quayside.

Grace looked out of the hotel window from beneath the eaves of the old thatched roof and pulled a face.

"No beach today then! What else is there to do in this boring place!"

The whole family had come on what was indeed an exciting journey; firstly by plane from Birmingham to Dublin, and then across lush green fields to Westport: a bustling seaside town, no doubt fabulous in the sunshine, but their hotel was right by the bay and despite the glorious views, in the teeming rain, even this charming building seemed cold and unwelcoming.

Grace's brother Michael was quite happy with his headphones on, sprawled across the window seat; but she grew restless and glared at her parents, quite happily engrossed in the newspapers that obscured them almost entirely from view.

"Can I go for a walk?" she ventured, knowing what the answer would be.

Before Grace's dad could deliver his safety speech, the hotel manager, Noreen, put her head around the heavy lounge door.

"I'm going up to Westport House," she said cheerily in her soft Irish accent. "Do you want me to show you around? It's exciting, even on a day like this."

They all agreed that this was a good idea, and after hurriedly putting on waterproofs and finding various weird umbrellas from the old stand in the hallway, they braved the elements, Michael still managing to keep his headphones on under his hood.

It was freezing considering it was August, the infuriating wind almost pushing them bodily along the seafront, and Noreen's auburn curly hair grew increasingly wild as it escaped from her comical waterproof hat.

"Well, it's a day for pirates to be sure!" she grinned, "and there's plenty of stories about them in these parts. One with your name on…" She winked at Grace.

When they got to the house, Mum, Dad and Grace became enthralled by its history, especially Grace who stood for ages by the blank-eyed white statue of Grace O'Malley and studied the fascinating information. She read everything twice while her brother turned up the volume on his headphones and tried not to yawn.

"What a tremendous character she was!" Noreen's eyes sparkled.

"A bit like our own Grace!" remarked Mum.

There seemed to be a break in the rain, so they all trooped out into the extensive grounds, the wet grass soaking their shoes. Grace lagged behind and noticed an intriguing sign which read *Pirates' Dungeon*. She stepped cautiously into the dimly lit passage, which led to another part of the house, laughing inwardly at the comical pictures of pirate characters on the wall.

But then she heard a strange noise, almost as if chains were being dragged along the floor, and a dull thumping sound. As she turned the corner it was like a scene from a film: a group of rough-looking men were heaving on a long, grimy rope and chain. They all seemed to be dressed in old-fashioned, extremely dirty clothes, and a tall, imposing woman – well, Grace thought it was a woman, although she was completely dressed in men's attire – strode among them, her bedraggled hair spilling out of the filthy pirate's hat that she wore.

"Liven up, you lazy oafs; we need to make the evening tide…"

She turned and stared coldly at Grace.

"And what are you gawping at? Get on the end of the line…"

Grace was pushed unceremoniously almost on top of a young lad probably about the same age as her brother.

"Just don't argue with her!" he grinned, his blackened teeth just visible in the dim light of the cavern-like corridor.

"But…!" Grace protested, "is it a film?"

"Shh! Get stuck in, ask questions later!" He settled in front of her and she felt she had to join him.

After what seemed like an age of pulling on the greasy rope, Grace slumped to the floor, exhausted.

"Who is she? What's going on?" Grace's questions fell on deaf ears.

There she was again: the formidable lady pirate issuing orders, clipping the younger lads around the ear.

Suddenly, Grace felt herself being hauled from the floor.

"Just because you're a girl don't think you can take it easy!"

"But I'm…!" Grace's voice tailed off as she came face to face with the Pirate Queen, for that's what she was.

"No food until it's finished!" she grinned at her. "What village are you from? Your face looks familiar!"

"Um… well, I'm from Coventry…"

"Never heard of it! Less talking, more action!"

Grace reluctantly hauled on the rope once more and then mercifully a loud bell sounded and everyone let go of it.

"Dinnertime!" grinned the young lad who had spoken to her earlier.

All the people rushed to the end of what appeared to be a long tunnel in front of them, but Grace hung back, uncertain. A pale mist seemed to follow them.

"Grace! There you are…"

Mum's call seemed to break the spell.

"What are you doing? Have you found something interesting?"

Grace muttered an excuse, suddenly not wanting to share the strange experience with her mum. She just linked arms with her, reassured by her presence.

*

They all spent the rest of the day learning about the connection between Westport House and the O'Malleys. Even Michael was interested in the swashbuckling pirate stories.

Grace flicked through the information leaflets in the shop on their way out of the house, trying to find details of filmmaking or a play being performed at the venue.

"Oh, no, sorry," said the young assistant when Grace made a tentative enquiry. "Nothing like that until next summer." She smiled in a friendly way, displaying slightly disconcerting bright green braces on her front teeth. "I'll email you the details if you like."

Grace stopped herself from asking any more awkward questions, but confided later in Noreen.

"Oh, Westport House has great links with the past," she whispered to her after dinner. "Those that are sensitive may well slip back in time."

Grace shuddered slightly, but grinned to herself and started to sketch the strong face with wild ringlets escaping from a pirate's hat.

"Ah, yes," smiled Noreen, "that's our Pirate Queen!"

Robin

For me, robins were always a sign of cheerfulness and homeliness; comforting and reliable, never fazed by people around them, sitting close by, observing steadily with a dark, shiny eye, ruffling their feathers; just a friend in the garden.

Although I think in reality they are not very nice to the other birds who trespass on their territory; but that kind of spoils their cosy image; so I will ignore this information.

I was taking a stroll across the city park in my lunch hour, working with my dad in the school holidays. It is a gorgeous place, dedicated to all those who lost their lives in the First and Second World Wars. There are trees planted carefully with little stone plaques, remembering these brave men who sadly died all those years ago.

Suddenly, out of the corner of my eye, I saw a robin fly very low to the ground and stop, as unafraid as ever, just under a hedge to the side of the path. I acknowledged it, but walked on. A few seconds later, it appeared again, higher up this time.

"How did you know it was the same one?" my friend asked much later. Well, I didn't, but it was fun to imagine so.

I had to pass along a rather muddy track, sheltered from the wind but not the rain – and there it was again; this time right in front of me. Intrigued, I got as close as I could; then it flew off, high into a nearby oak tree, a little further ahead to the right. It almost seemed as if it expected me to follow it. So I couldn't stop myself; and before I knew it I was in a part of the park that I hadn't been to before.

The cheeky bird had vanished and, to be quite honest, I felt a bit vulnerable in this dark walkway. So I turned back to retrace my steps, but realised that I was completely lost.

Trying not to panic, I ran as far as the path could take me, then – nothing. A dead end. So I ran the other way, a bit upset by now. But there it was again – the robin, flying steadily ahead then swerving to the right, disappearing into thick undergrowth. I stepped through gingerly to avoid horrid stinging nettles and then my feet knocked against something solid. It was so dark I just had to feel to see what it was. My fingers closed on a rectangular, smooth object; then I found a handle. A case, maybe?

Thoughts of bombs and other unmentionable things made me hesitant, but curiosity got the better of me and I pulled hard, dragging what was indeed an old leather suitcase back onto the path.

And there was the robin again, quietly looking at me from a tree stump nearby.

I clicked the rusty fasteners, not really expecting it to open, but they shot back and – very gingerly– I raised the lid.

As I did so, a warm breeze stirred the undergrowth and the robin flew off – but not very far, I guessed.

I peered inside and saw a whole host of things packed tightly together. Old photos of people in uniform; a ration book, complete with coupons; an old-fashioned lamp; a notebook; a packet of cigarettes; small silver binoculars; an army knife; and a dark brown leather wallet stuffed with notes!

I gasped and sat back on my heels, feeling as if I were

intruding into someone's private life, only pausing to look at a dog-eared 'Ovaltineys' membership card.

No mobile phone. I wasn't lucky enough to own one yet, so I clicked the fasteners shut and tried to find my way back to the main park, carefully carrying the case.

The robin had rejoined me, flying from branch to branch as if to reassure me that I was going the right way.

*

Dad and I took it later to the nearest police station. It turned out to belong to an old soldier whose family lived in the city. I wondered why it had been hidden in the park.

On closer inspection by the soldier's family, they found a tattered envelope with a beautifully handwritten letter inside. It was addressed to his brother...

... And so I am sorry for the arguments we had. I hope you will forgive me. Here is the money I had left and Mum's special ring...

Attached to the letter was a little linen pouch with the most beautiful sapphire and diamond ring inside. When the family took it to the soldier's brother, in his nineties now and being looked after in a care home, slow tears trickled down his heavily-lined face.

"We fell out, you know, before he went to war. The last time I heard from him was when he sent me this..." He drew out a small creased card, blank inside save for one word:

Sorry

"This is as close as I could get to shaking his hand. He was killed in action."

On the front of the card was a blurry picture of a small bird. A robin.

Running Away

Michael found writing difficult. In fact, he found everything difficult: reading, maths, science; even art seemed frustrating. He couldn't sing in tune and he hated making models. Computer work never went well. But there was one lesson where he felt at ease and in control – PE. Michael had a natural ability for sport – a good footballer, bounding with energy – in fact, he could play any ball game successfully. But his real talent was running; he just kept going, and fast. When he was running he didn't have to worry. Everything was natural, easy; he didn't have to struggle.

One of the teachers at his primary school ran a cross-country club and as soon as he got to Year 3 he went along just to see what it was all about.

"Two laps of the field," shouted Miss Coleman, her red hair whipping across her face in the sharp wind. "It doesn't matter how fast you go, walk if you can't keep up the pace!"

Walk? No chance! Naturally competitive, Michael went to the front. The older children let him through – after all, this young Year 3 boy would soon get tired, so they thought! But Michael's skinny legs just went faster and faster. Suddenly, they all realised no one was going to catch him. Miss Coleman stood amidst the damp grass, literally open-

mouthed. Here was a real talent – such a surprise too, given his many problems with other areas of school.

Michael was oblivious to the children running behind him; pure joy shone from his young face, he was just totally focused on getting to the line before anyone else. As he approached Miss Coleman with her clipboard, he did glance over his shoulder and even surprised himself when he saw how much he was in front; the Year 6 boys were at least 50 metres behind, sweat plastering their hair to their heads.

"Michael! Well done – you are certainly in the team for a week next Saturday. Do your parents know how fast you can run?"

"Dunno, they've never seen me…" Michael pretended to fiddle with his laces, embarrassed by the attention.

"Huh, I'm sure he didn't go round twice!" Alex Sumner was still suffering from stitch.

"Oh, he did, Alex," Miss Coleman smiled. "I saw him!"

So Michael took home a letter that evening to say that he had been chosen for the cross-country team and there was a competition in the next couple of weeks.

"Running?!" Michael's dad frowned, "I don't know about that, it might interfere with football training." Dad was an enthusiastic children's coach and ran the under 10's local team.

"But it will make me even fitter." Michael fidgeted from one foot to another. He desperately wanted to go to the competition, but knew that in Dad's eyes football came first above everything else.

"I'll look at the fixture list, let's see…"

Michael's fingers were crossed behind his back as his dad scanned the list on the kitchen wall.

"Well, luckily, there's nothing on that day – I suppose it will be okay, but if it affects your performance…"

Michael pushed the consent form in front of him and his dad signed it almost reluctantly.

His mum was more enthusiastic, especially when she realised how excited Michael was.

"I was good, Mum," Michael whispered to her.

"I bet you were!" She hugged him fiercely. She knew her son had huge learning problems. It was good to celebrate his successes, no matter how small.

*

All the cross-country team were taken by Miss Coleman later that week for a special training session. It should have been her afternoon when she had time for planning and assessment, but she gave it up readily, realising how important it was for them to perform well, especially children like Michael.

Released from their ordinary PE lessons, they were all doing shuttle runs across the playground. Michael, again, way ahead of everyone else.

"Miss Coleman!" a loud voice shouted across the adjoining grass. "Is Michael Levitt with you?"

Michael's heart sank. Mrs Richardson, the teaching assistant, had come to take him to extra reading sessions which were held on Fridays.

Miss Coleman took a deep breath and shook her head.

"No, this is too important – I'll make up his time next lunchtime!"

Poor Mrs Richardson; she knew Michael didn't want to go and she hated asking, but his reading was so weak.

"Well, he'll have to come next time – we have to do assessments…"

Mrs Richardson wrote in her notebook and Michael, relieved, yelled: "I'll do some practice at home…"

They all knew that he wouldn't.

*

The day of the race arrived and, to Michael's surprise, his dad decided to come and watch as well as Mum. He felt really nervous. What if he was sick? What if he didn't get near the front? His heart thumped as they walked from the car park to the meeting point at the edge of the course.

The Year 6 crowd only made him feel worse. Trying to be kind and supportive, they kept telling each other how good he was and how he was going to beat everyone.

Then he spotted the smart running kit of the local private school. Most of them were members of the nearest athletics club, all following slick warm-up routines and looking deadly serious.

"Oh, don't mind them," smiled Miss Coleman, pinning his number to his rather faded vest. "You're just as good!" He wasn't so sure.

Checking his laces for the hundredth time, he lined up at the start in the squelchy mud. Everyone was jostling for a good position.

"Just go at your own pace," Miss Coleman patted his shoulder. "Enjoy it, Michael." He could just see Mum waving frantically; his dad frowning, hands deep in his pockets.

Then they were off. Michael almost tripped in the rush, but managed to stay on his feet somehow. They had to run around yellow markers. The most difficult thing was that the spectators, eager to get a better view, were actually in the way of the runners, despite the marshals trying to push them back.

Michael kept his eyes on two of the private school boys at the front, but then it got very confusing and he wasn't sure which way to go. He almost stopped, looking wildly about him. Then, thankfully, he saw Miss Coleman.

"No, that way, Michael!" She ran alongside him for a while.

It was no good, he'd gone too wide and the leaders were way out in front. Why did he always mess things up? – his chance to prove himself.

As he eventually reached the 'funnel' at the end of the race, Miss Coleman was waiting.

"You did so well!" she beamed at him.

7th said the crumpled blue card in his sweaty hand. It might as well have been 37th!

Mum came rushing up, full of praise.

"Where did you come then?" asked Dad unsmiling. Michael shoved the card towards him. Now he'd stop him going to the school club, because he hadn't won. Michael hung his head and shuffled his feet.

To his amazement, Dad lifted him bodily into the air.

"You, young man, are an amazing runner, and you did so well to make up the ground when you went the wrong way. We'd better get you to a proper running club then!"

Miss Coleman stood nearby, tears in her eyes. Job done.

*

Michael, with his family's support and extra coaching from Miss Coleman, easily won his next race. He even found the time and inclination to practise his reading. His new-found confidence and belief in himself extended into other areas of school, and so Mrs Richardson took him off her list.

"You'd probably only run away from me, Michael!" she laughed as he slipped a new library book into his bag and sped off to cross-country practice.

Shadows – That's All

"Why on earth are you crying so much?"

Sean's mum had finally run out of patience. Normally understanding and softly spoken, this evening she felt drained from a hard day teaching lively Year 6 pupils.

Now her own usually placid, easily soothed little boy showed no signs of going back to sleep, and it was already 10pm. The six-year-old's cries just grew louder by the minute. His dad issued various threats from downstairs as to what would happen if the awful sound of crying didn't stop.

"Well, that's not helping," muttered Mum through gritted teeth.

Going against all her own private rules, she lifted the sobbing child out of his dishevelled duvet, its brightly coloured train pattern just visible in the light of the street lamp outside.

"Now what's the matter, what's bothering you?" she whispered into his ear, hugging his small, sweaty body closely to her.

"It's the shadows – that's all…" Sean glanced fearfully over her shoulder and sobbed again.

Mum peered out into the silent suburban street and realised what he meant. The crooked bare winter branches of the young horse chestnut tree which stood in the front garden

were waving as if in a frenzy, for an unusually strong wind was gusting all around the house. The street light shone eerily through it, making strange patterns on the bedroom wall.

"Oh, Sean, it's only the conker tree dancing in the wind!" She tried to sound cheery despite her tiredness. But he was having none of it and continued to cling to her.

She sighed, cursing the fact that she'd taken down the blackout curtains for winter, and thinking of the pile of undone marking downstairs. She'd have to get up even earlier in the morning to do it.

The tree had grown strongly from a conker that they'd planted almost as soon as Sean could walk, despite Dad saying that there was no way a tree could grow "just like that" from a conker tipped haphazardly into a shallow hole. But strong green shoots had appeared and a few years later a young sapling stood, now jigging about like a dancer rooted to the spot. They had planted a time capsule underneath – a plastic box with photos, small toys, scribbled notes and an old-fashioned cassette tape with Sean's first words recorded onto it.

So mother and son cuddled up together on the old wooden rocking chair and the shadows continued to dance on the wall.

*

It must have been around three in the morning when Mum woke up with a start. Sean was sleeping peacefully now, eyes fluttering in some vivid dream. She lifted him off her lap and settled him into bed, yawning wearily. She might just get a few hours…

Then the tapping started.

It sounded for all the world like someone playing a snare drum, but very badly. Annoyed, thinking a silly teenager or even an animal was messing about outside, Mum looked out. Was it her imagination or did the tree seem closer to the house than usual? The branches were indeed touching the window like stretched-out crabby fingers.

Now don't be so ridiculous, she thought to herself. *You just need some sleep.*

The tapping persisted. Any minute now and surely Sean would wake up. Maybe if she could push the offending branch away...

The sound became more regular and louder – tap, tap-tap, tap.

Mum gingerly opened the window and gave a small gasp as the icy air touched her face. She reached out her hand and caught a knobbly branch, pushing it away as strongly as she could. The shadow on the wall was now still – how strange!

She shut the window carefully, trying not to wake Sean who snored, stirred and turned over.

But the tapping still went on.

The stairs were in complete blackness and, not wanting to wake anyone, she resisted even putting on the downstairs light. A full moon almost brazenly shone through the landing window, forming more deep, solid shadows below her.

The house keys glinted in the moonlight from their hook in the hall and she was easily able to find the ones for the front door. It was always a stiff lock but it swung away from her at last and she stepped out onto the gravel driveway.

Overhead, a sudden clump of clouds blotted out the moon and she stumbled over the edge of the grass, pulling her thin dressing gown around her.

The noise couldn't be heard from here, but the tree still creaked and swayed in the wind. So was that what was making the noise, or was it something else?

Then the clouds parted and the moon appeared timidly, in the silvery light. Her eyes were drawn to a disturbed mound of earth close to the trunk of the horse chestnut. It was the exact spot where Sean's time capsule had been buried. Maybe an animal had dug it up. Then Mum saw that indeed a trail of things lay across the path. All those little mementoes just tossed around in the dirt. It made her cross.

She peered into the hole and realised that the old plastic box was there, but with the top seemingly wrenched off. Strangely, the old cassette tape was still inside it.

After she had picked up all the contents of the box from the grass, she stuffed the tape into her pocket, covered the hole over and went back to the welcoming warmth of the house. She was so tired she didn't even notice that the noise had stopped.

*

It wasn't until the weekend, when she was sorting through the mounds of washing, that she found the cassette tape again. Wondering if it still worked, she rooted out her old cassette player and slotted the still slightly damp tape into the machine.

She pressed *play*.

There was Sean's shaky voice giggling through a muddled message. But there again was another sound, another voice: "Will you come and play when you're older? I'll tap the window to let you know when I'm here."

Shepherd's Lane

Whenever Mum drove down Shepherd's Lane in the dark, she would always check that the orange locking light was showing, and if by any chance it wasn't, she would snap it on quickly and look almost nervously in the rearview mirror.

She didn't think that we noticed; but we knew that she didn't like driving down here at night. Me, my younger brother and sister, usually chatting away in the back; but I always saw that little action, and felt her nervousness.

"We don't like it down here!" three-year-old Florence piped up one evening as we were driving back from visiting our cousins in Birmingham.

"Don't be silly, Florence," said Dad automatically, checking the football scores on his mobile.

"We don't like it!" echoed Hugo, my entertaining brother, who opened his eyes wide in mock horror and pressed his sticky hands on the side window as he peered out into the night.

"Maicie said the trees are weird!" he continued.

I glowered at him, knowing I'd be in trouble for scaring them both.

"Yes, they're all monsters that come to life at night and eat children… aaagh!" Dad screwed round from the front seat, his white teeth glinting briefly as they passed the first and only lamppost.

We all giggled. Dad was confident and reassuring, and totally 'over the top' so that he dispelled our fears to a certain extent; but I, the oldest, could see why Mum felt a bit uncomfortable as she negotiated the potholes and bends in this eerie country lane.

The moon slipped out from behind the blanket of thick dark clouds, and certainly the trees lining the road were the strangest of shapes: crooked right from the bottom with thick ugly branches that were raised up like threatening arms. In the darkness they looked almost as if they were giant-like figures, peering at the cars passing by.

It was a different story in the daytime or early evening. We often passed that way as soft orange sunsets burst through these very trees from the fields on both sides of the road – a kind of filtered light which made the whole area seem dream-like.

Last Sunday, Dad took me on one of his famous country walks. Mum stayed with the younger two as they went to swimming lessons and so I had the luxury of Dad's full attention for a couple of hours.

I'm sure he didn't mean to go down Shepherd's Lane but we often got lost on his spontaneous ventures and suddenly I realised with a jolt exactly where we were.

It was a beautiful calm, sunny day; a heat haze lay across the fields and you could clearly hear the birdsong. As usual, very little traffic passed by, but all the same I stayed close to Dad, until he stopped after hobbling awkwardly.

"Ouch, I must have a stone in my boot. I think it's giving me a blister. Carry on to that oak tree and wait; it's safe there. Go on, there's not room for two of us to stand safely here."

He could see I was reluctant to go on my own.

I took a deep breath and, glowering back at him, hummed loudly to myself as I approached the ancient tree, only a few metres ahead of me.

Suddenly, a soft-eared grey rabbit appeared from the hedgerow, looked round with startled eyes and disappeared again. I bent down to see where it had gone. As I did, I tripped over a stone and fell towards the trunk. Astonishingly, there appeared to be a small metal handle attached to it.

Intrigued now, and forgetting my fears, I pulled at it and to my surprise, no, almost horror, the whole trunk opened to strangely reveal a kind of tunnel.

I looked back at Dad through the open doorway and could see he was still fiddling with his boot.

"I'm just looking in here!" I shouted, but he didn't even raise his head. I felt almost drawn to the small space and found myself crawling along an earthy floor. I looked back nervously again, just about seeing the bright blue sky behind me.

Ahead, there appeared to be another brightness, and eventually I found myself in a large cavern-like place with a central fire burning in an old-fashioned brazier. I was tempted just to turn and scramble back; but again something drew me towards the flames.

From the shadows at the back of the cavern I heard a slight movement. Frightened again, I backed away. But then I saw a girl of about the same age as me, perhaps nine or ten, in a curiously long dress and a dirty apron.

"Hello," she spoke timidly, "who are you?"

"Maicie." I didn't know what else to say.

"Where've you been?" The girl looked at me sideways.

"Shepherd's Lane."

"Oh, the other side."

"The other side of where?"

"Don't know, we're not allowed out there!" She held out a bony arm. "Come and see my friends."

Two other children appeared: a boy, much taller with strange, ragged trousers and a smaller girl who hid behind the boy's legs.

They led me past the fire – how odd on a hot summer's

day – down a rocky pathway to a kind of enclosed garden area with a makeshift swing and a kind of garden hut or shed.

"What's that for?" I asked. I was curious, despite still being nervous.

"Oh, the shepherd's hut," the girl replied. "He's not here today because he's out, up on the top fields. Good job; he's a bit peculiar, doesn't like children…"

It seemed rude to ask any more questions.

So we played on the swing and they showed me an old-fashioned game called 'Five Stones'. As we sat on the floor I realised it was really cold, even frosty, and yet when I was walking down the lane with Dad it had been a hot summer's day… Dad! He'd be really annoyed and worried by now!

"I've got to go!" I said hurriedly. "My dad, he'll be extremely cross; he's in the lane…"

"Will he beat you?" the girl asked quietly.

"No!" I replied, again curious to hear her say that.

So I waved goodbye and crawled as quickly as I could down the low-ceilinged tunnel back to the warm summer's day I'd left behind.

Amazingly, Dad was there, seemingly still fiddling with his boot.

"I'm okay!" I shouted to him from across the road.

"I know you are!" he laughed. "You've only been out of sight for a minute; are you playing hide and seek?"

I didn't reply, but looked back at the oak tree. The handle seemed to have disappeared. I went back and felt all around it. Nothing.

"What are you looking for?" Dad was mildly amused.

"Oh, it doesn't matter…"

*

I'd read about time slips but really didn't believe in them and tried to put the whole experience down to my very vivid imagination, so that it became like a half-remembered dream.

It wasn't until the following week that we drove that way again. I was in the back seat and, as we passed by the same crooked oak tree, the moonlight shone right onto its rough trunk and I could just see the very door which I had gone through before. It was entirely… open.

Stick With It

They said that he would only have to have the special leg splints on for six weeks; but already it was three months and he was still no better. Tariq lifted his crutches wearily. It was so very hot; everything hurt, he couldn't play football – in fact, he couldn't play anything, except chess, and that was okay, but his friends didn't like it much. Everyone was kind at first, helping him with his heavy school bags and lunchboxes; but little by little, people got tired of this and forgot to do things, so that he had to keep asking – which was so embarrassing.

Tariq, normally a sunny-natured boy, became a little bit moody, sulky even, and certainly impatient.

"It's not fair!" he moaned to his mum one Friday. "I'll miss Sports Day and everything!"

"Go and see if you can walk steadily to the shops and treat yourself to an ice cream," she said kindly. "You can sit on the bench to eat it." It was a long time since he had had the operation and the doctor had, in truth, been worried about his progress. She tried not to show her concerns to her despondent young son.

So he made his way gingerly to the local shop, only perhaps 200 metres away, but it took him a good ten minutes to struggle there.

The last house before the shop belonged to a certain Inge De Burgh, a German lady in her mid eighties, who despite living in this country since she was a teenager retained a strong accent. Tariq always had a smile for her, and, despite his dull mood, today was no exception. She was full of character with her 'no-nonsense' approach and hearty laughter. As he passed her front garden, she was there, leaning on a brightly coloured walking stick, trying her best to weed the path and becoming increasingly frustrated when she couldn't reach properly.

Tariq paused by the rough stone wall.

"Hello, Mrs De Burgh! You and I are in the same boat, I think!"

"Huh! Well, at least you are going to get better, young man – as for me…" She straightened up, grabbing another stick which hung from a branch overhead so that she was steadier.

"Have you bought a new walking stick?" Tariq momentarily forgot his own discomfort, pointing to the shiny blue one in her left hand.

"Oh no," she replied, composing a serious face. "I've got a stick tree. I grow them in the garden!"

Tariq stared at her. He was ten in a couple of months' time, and therefore considered himself too old for such stories. But with Mrs De Burgh – well, she always insisted on being absolutely honest and straightforward.

"What do you mean?" Tariq was fascinated. "Do you make them yourself?"

"Oh no, I plant stick seeds in the ground and in no time at all a new tree pops up with young sticks growing on it!"

Her deep brown eyes crinkled into a smile.

"They need a lot of watering, though!"

Tariq didn't really believe her, and yet she had never made things up before…

He said his goodbyes, managed to buy himself a huge red lolly from the shop, ate it on the wooden bench which was conveniently outside and, as he was struggling back along the pavement, he noticed Mrs De Burgh had gone in, but two brand new sticks were swinging from the lower branches of a tree, knocking against each other in the breeze. He grinned inwardly to himself.

To Tariq's mum's delight, from that day on he made a point of passing the 'stick tree' every day. Sure enough, each time he saw a new one, sometimes half-hidden amongst the fat dark green leaves.

*

Later that week, the doctor said after his routine examination that it would be at least another three months before Tariq could get rid of his crutches. When they got home, he threw them angrily across the living room floor, terrifying the cat and worrying his mum.

"Now look, there's nothing we can do about it," she spoke gently. "Just do all the exercises and you will build up your strength in no time."

Tariq wasn't so sure. Maybe he'd always have to walk with a stick, like Mrs De Burgh…

The next day, he and his mum were driving past Mrs De Burgh's house when he noticed a distinctive yellow stick swinging from the front of the tree. A total of six others were suspended from the branches, but he had never seen this one before.

Later that afternoon, as he limped along the uneven pavement once more, he saw that Mrs De Burgh was grappling with a long, slippery green hosepipe.

"That's a brilliant new stick, Mrs De Burgh!" called Tariq.

"Oh yes, quite rare!" she coughed as she spoke, "I shan't pick it, though, until it's ripe. This one has healing qualities!"

Again really unsure as to whether to take her seriously, Tariq carefully crossed over the road.

"Shall I help you with that?"

He somehow clumsily got through the little wrought iron gate and held one end of the hosepipe with his free hand, while she watered the hydrangeas.

"Come back on Friday, it should be ripe enough then," she whispered mysteriously and tapped the side of her nose. "I'll know when it's ready."

"When it's ready for what?" Tariq was curious but almost didn't like to ask too many questions; she could be a bit fierce sometimes.

"Patience, young man, patience!"

She turned to go back inside, grabbing a bright emerald green stick as she did so, which again he hadn't seen before.

*

So, on Friday, Tariq went straight round from school to Mrs De Burgh's house. She was nowhere to be seen; but by the gate was the bright yellow stick he had seen earlier with a splendid bronze stripe down one side. It had a label attached to it which read:

For Tariq. Use this to exercise with, at least twice every day, and it will help you to get better.

Looking around him, he knocked at the front door to thank her; but there was no answer. So, almost guiltily, he managed to take the stick back to his house by stuffing it in his rucksack and carrying it on his back while he managed the crutches.

And so every day he would use the yellow stick to walk around the garden with, instead of the dreadful crutches, and he used it while doing his exercises. Two months later at his regular check-up his doctor was mystified.

"Well, Tariq, you have surprised me!" he said, scratching his head. "In all honesty I really didn't think I would be saying this so soon, but I think we can do away with your splints now!"

"It was the yellow stick, you see," Tariq spoke matter-of-factly. "It has healing qualities, you know."

"And what stick would that be?" The doctor was bemused.

"Oh, it's one of Mrs De Burgh's. She grows walking sticks in her garden and this is the one she picked for me; she said it would help me to get better!"

"Well, you just tell Mrs De Burgh it has certainly worked!" The doctor raised his eyebrows but smiled.

As soon as they got home Tariq asked his mum to drop him off near Mrs De Burgh's house.

He made his way carefully up the garden path, trying to get used to walking without the supports he had borne for so long. However, he soon noticed all the curtains were closed and more importantly there were no sticks on the tree.

He lifted the shiny brass knocker and let it fall tentatively against the faded blue front door. He wasn't really expecting an answer as the place looked deserted; but eventually it creaked open. There was Mrs De Burgh looking smart in her best hat and coat, surrounded by packing cases.

"I'm glad you've called." She gestured for him to come in. "As you can see, I'm on the move!"

They chatted for some time and Tariq told her about his marvellously unexpected recovery.

"Well now, that is good news!" Her face lit up. "I'm going to live with my daughter, so I perhaps won't see you again, but I'd very much like you to have these." She handed him a long brown envelope labelled shakily in pencil: *Stick Seeds*.

*

They never did grow into stick trees – just beautiful wild flowers; but Tariq insisted that all their stems were really straight; and they certainly cheered up everyone who took time to appreciate them if they went out for a nice long walk…

Superheroes!

"But I don't think I want to go!"

Holly screwed up her reddening face and buried her head under her creased pillow with its glittery pattern.

It was a week before she was due to go away with her Year 6 field trip. "A treat," the teachers had said. "A reward for all your hard work."

More like an endurance test! thought Holly. She was perpetually nervous and worried about new situations – Mum and Dad thought it was a good idea and at first Holly went along with it; choosing friends to share her room with, buying new trainers and a cool waterproof – but now it was only three days away, all too real.

They'd been to the parents' information evening; asked lots of questions and Holly seemed to be settled about the arrangements. But now it WAS going to happen. Five whole nights without Mum and Dad…

Somehow they finally managed to persuade their timid daughter to turn up at the gate on departure day, complete with oversized case, bulging rucksack, massive packed lunch and a slightly scruffy teddy – well, the boys were bringing them too!

Flustered teachers ticked off names, ushered people in and out of the toilet and finally everyone was on the coach ready to go. For two pins, Holly would run back down the aisle and scream "Let me off!" But her cheery friend Gemma was talking non-stop and anyway the coach had started to move. Mum and Dad were soon dots in the distance. Holly was sure Mum had been crying too…

*

The journey took ages; but eventually the huge coach started to climb steeper, narrower roads; they were actually in Wales. Everyone, it seemed, felt sick, apart from Holly; wonder of wonders! She handed mints to Gemma who by now had her head almost inside the plastic bag on her lap.

At least she's stopped talking! thought Holly and grinned to herself. Well, she wasn't the worst this time – at least at travelling.

Eventually, they arrived seemingly in the middle of nowhere and everyone walked through mounds of sheep poo to the low grey house set against a beautiful backdrop of hills and pine trees.

It was unnervingly quiet. They all stood gathered round the gate while they were welcomed to the centre.

The evening passed in a flurry of unpacking, practice fire drills and a welcome meal in the tightly packed dining room with its lumpy white plastered walls and ancient fireplace.

Holly was so tired that she didn't really give home a thought. She was just intent on keeping up with everything that was going on.

As she was brushing her teeth alongside the other girls, the wobbly tooth that had threatened to drop out for the last few days flipped onto the side of the sink.

"Hey!" grinned Gemma, who still looked slightly green. "Tell Mrs Timms!"

The experienced teaching assistant, so familiar with the routine of these residential visits, took time out from cajoling the excited group of girls to appreciate how important this was to Holly.

"Now you just give that to me, we'll find an envelope and leave it for the Welsh fairies."

Sean Brown, passing in the nearby corridor, caught the end of this conversation and made a scoffing noise, stopping immediately as Mrs Timms glared at him.

*

Such excitement next morning. Everyone crowded round to see the envelope, covered with rather primitive drawings of 'Welsh' fairies and containing a shiny pound coin. Sean Brown smirked again.

"You're just jealous!" Holly grinned. She thought she might like it here after all.

Their first activity was to be a mountain walk.

"All day?" Holly asked Jude, the group leader, incredulously.

The strong, young teacher smiled warmly at her and showed them all the route they would be taking on a large plastic-covered wall map.

"Where's the toilets?" Holly was a frequent bathroom visitor.

"In the bushes!" laughed Jude. "Now come on, you have fifteen minutes to get ready."

As they made their way along the narrow roads in the

brand new minibus, determined splashes of rain began to fall.

"Waterproofs on!" ordered Jude cheerily as they bundled out onto the stony path. "We'll start inside the mountain while the weather is bad.

For Holly it was her worst nightmare. They all trooped right into the heart of the mountain. Even though they had 'headlights' strapped to their helmets, Holly's tiny feet constantly tripped over unseen rocks and potholes. She clung onto Mrs Timms and heaved a huge sigh of relief when they eventually found daylight.

Jude checked the weather outside.

"Well, it's raining all right – but I am sure it's easing off."

Famous last words.

The whole group of ten stepped out blinking into the terrible weather. Within minutes they were all soaked. It was bitterly cold, and the worst thing was the wind. Holly was so light it seemed as if she would be lifted right off the mountainside, rucksack and all.

Some of the 'tougher' boys were visibly shaken. Sean Brown pretended to be wiping his glasses, but Holly knew he was really crying.

"It's okay, Sean," Holly shouted into the wind, "use your hands like me!" She found that she could make her way down the slippery slates like a mountain goat on all fours.

Sean remained rigid, petrified of moving. Holly stopped, sympathising with his fear. She hoisted her rucksack more securely onto her back and made her way up to where he was clinging to a slippery tree stump.

"Look, hold onto me. We'll go together!"

Her voice was lost in the wind, but Sean gratefully

grabbed onto her small arm and gingerly followed her down the steep pathway.

The adults were waiting at a more level part, near a broken-down old miner's cottage. Holly, sensitive towards people's feelings by the looks on their faces, could see they were worried too. But with newly gained confidence and with a huge effort, she pulled Sean closer to her and they made it to a small grassy verge.

"Good gracious, Holly!" exclaimed Mrs Timms. "You're being SO brave!"

Holly just grinned and pushed her dripping straight hair further under her oversized helmet.

"Oh, Sean and I were helping each other," she said generously.

Everyone returned at last to the shelter of the minibus and when they were all queuing for welcome hot showers back at the centre, Holly overheard a conversation going on in the staffroom next door: "Well, I was a bit worried there!" – clearly Jude's voice – "but did you see Holly Jeavons? What a superhero, who would have thought it…?"

Holly hugged herself inwardly – a superhero! Something to be proud of, for sure.

The Hidden

The twins raced down the raised sandy path towards Kenilworth Castle which stood proud and imposing against the brilliant blue sky; almost like a jigsaw puzzle piece slotted into position against this perfect backdrop.

It was the very first day of the long school holidays; six weeks of freedom called. Not that this pair didn't enjoy school. Both sociable in their different ways: Simon adventurous and, well, generally louder as his mum would often observe; Steven more imaginative, creative and dreamy, full of laid-back good humour.

They had both looked forward to this trip for a fortnight. "A reward for staying out of trouble all year," Nan smiled as she handed them the entrance fee. "No, I'm not coming – you'll only get me playing hide-and-seek…"

So just the three of them arrived at the gatehouse and studied the floor plans carefully.

"Well, I'll look after the lunch, you two are big enough to explore on your own." Mum hoisted their giant rucksacks from their sweaty shoulders and set up her striped folding chair. *Half an hour to sit and sketch*, she thought to herself, being a talented artist, but not finding much time in between her part-time job at the local school and looking after her energetic offspring. She sighed a little. Once she had dreamt of a creative career. Still, maybe her time would come. For the moment she was happy to take on the odd commission. She could sketch the castle; it might come in handy and it was a lovely thing to do on a perfect day like this.

Simon sped up the nearest grassy bank and Steven, already red-faced, tried in vain to overtake.

"Bloomin' kids!" muttered a disgruntled elderly gentleman in a creased linen suit as the twins narrowly avoided him, but he couldn't help smiling to himself and remembering his own boyhood days in this very spot, as he sat down unsteadily on a convenient bench.

Every rickety staircase was ascended, every shadowy corner investigated; it was as if they had to make the most of every minute.

"Carpe Diem!" their wise teacher had told them. "Seize the day; don't be lazy in the holidays, use the time to feed your soul!"

The brothers were in no danger of leading boring lives – feeding their souls? Well, it wasn't long until lunchtime!

By twelve o'clock they were both ravenous and they finished their game of pretending to be captured in the cold, spooky cellar next to the ancient kitchens and ran over to Mum who was bent over her sketchpad, pretty dark blonde hair almost covering her work.

"Let's look – genius!" Steven especially was very proud of her, although it wasn't cool to tell her outright.

She pushed him away affectionately, snapped her bound book shut and started to dole out huge sandwiches.

"After lunch we could go to Leicester's Gatehouse," she suggested – "and I expect it's haunted…"

Steven particularly loved ghost stories and immediately

started to describe graphic torture scenes which he had thought of in the cellar.

"Oh, lay off, Steve; I've just got to the tomato sauce in my sandwich!" spluttered Simon. They all roared with laughter.

Lunch finished, Mum led them up to Leicester's Gatehouse, now beautifully furnished; gloomy, atmospheric and full of exciting artefacts. They spent a full half-hour in there; even Simon felt intrigued by the history of the place.

"Right, I'm off to the Stable Cafe for a cuppa," Mum announced. "I'll meet you in the Tudor garden at four; don't get lost in the maze!"

Steven wanted to look at the strange pink aviary near to the exterior wall of this fabulous recreated Elizabethan garden. Simon followed him good-naturedly, only pausing to flick his brother with water from the imposing fountain in the centre.

For a moment the sun went behind a lone cloud and the whole mood of the garden seemed to change. As they were peering at the delicate finches inside the aviary, Steven felt a hand on his shoulder. Startled, he turned around and saw a boy perhaps a year younger than him, looking rather frightened. He was very pale and extremely thin. Simon turned to see him too and afterwards remarked how scruffy his clothes were, something he would have never normally noticed – and he had bare feet.

"Do you want to play?" the boy asked almost nervously, looking behind him as he spoke.

"Of course!" Simon smiled at him good-naturedly. "We were just about to do hide-and-seek."

The boy nodded then said something strange: "That's good, but not by the kitchens, they might wake up."

"Who?" said both twins together.

"The cooks, of course; you don't want to rouse them mid-slumber…"

Puzzled, but unperturbed, they sorted out a game of hide-and-seek. Their new friend was remarkably good and seemed to know lots of fascinating hiding places that you wouldn't normally have noticed.

Puffing and panting, they all paused by the fountain and the boy unceremoniously scooped up some water into his cupped hands to quench his thirst. Simon screwed his face up.

"Won't that be mucky? Here, have some Coke." He fished out a decidedly warm bottle from his pocket. The boy sipped it and spat it straight out. Steven laughed.

"Don't blame you!" he giggled. "Bet it tastes like washing-up water!"

"Better go," the boy suddenly interrupted their laughter. He pointed at the sundial. "Almost time to get dinner ready and next month, of course, I won't have time to play at all, what with the Queen's visit and everything."

"The Queen's coming here?" Steven was fascinated.

"Well, you must be the only person round here that doesn't know about that!" The boy scratched his arm and Steven couldn't help noticing that it was covered in bruises.

"Hey, what happened to you?"

"Oh, that's nothing to what I'll get if I'm late!"

He pulled his sleeve down hurriedly.

"See you again maybe?" and with that he was off, his skinny legs taking him in the direction of the old kitchens; then he seemed to disappear in the heat haze.

Almost immediately, Mum appeared with ice creams. It wasn't until they were trudging back along the sandy path, the last to be let out of the castle grounds, that they told her about their new playmate.

"Queen's visit?" Mum was puzzled. "Not that I know of – he didn't mean Queen Elizabeth I?" She laughed, but screwed up her eyes thoughtfully.

As they drove past the gatehouse the sun had started to sink lower towards the height of this imposing castle. Steven looked back at the ramparts and was sure he could see a slight figure waving from one of the narrow windows…

The Visitors

It was just an ordinary Tuesday night like any other. Homework done and the tea being cooked; delicious smells coming from the kitchen. Daniel laid the table hurriedly – everyone in the house having a job to do. "Good training for life," Mum enthused. This evening she was stirring a giant pot of traditional Polish *'Bigos'*, a delicious meat stew. Her son's mouth watered. He was starving as always.

"Draw the curtains, will you!" Her voice came from the kitchen, just audible above the sound of 1970s disco music. Mum taught keep-fit classes and was forever working out some routine or other, usually at the same time as doing boring domestic chores.

Persistent rain trickled down the windows and Daniel released the tie-backs, taking care not to disturb his older sister Kasia's strange pottery piece, which she was so proud of. He secretly thought it looked like some kind of alien and seemed to grin at him in the bright light of the street lamp outside.

Then he saw it.

An acidic green light hovered over the maisonettes on the other side of the road. It was really intense, but flickering at the same time as it was turning in mid-air.

Daniel rubbed his eyes, but when he looked again it was still there.

"Mum!" he shouted, his nose pressed against the glass.

She didn't hear him, the music and the extractor fan drowning his voice.

Without warning, as he stared, the light shot up absolutely vertically and then sped off to the right, completely vanishing.

Daniel continued to stare at the night sky, but there was nothing more to see. He ran to the front door, opened it and looked down the street. Nothing except an elderly lady taking a bedraggled dog for a walk.

"Ooh, it's freezing!" Daniel shut the door just as Kasia ran down the stairs two at a time.

"Guess what I've just seen," he whispered to her. "I think it was a UFO!"

Kasia laughed and ruffled his spiky hair.

"You have got such a vivid imagination." She made a face. "Did you see an alien like this…?"

*

At dinner they all discussed what he thought he'd seen. Obviously, nobody believed him; Kasia was right, he was a very imaginative boy, writing short stories or plays and sharing them with anyone he could persuade to listen. Uncharacteristically, he became rather upset when Dad, who'd only just arrived home, tired and hungry, just laughed and asked him whether he'd spotted a spaceship in the supermarket car park next door.

Daniel stamped upstairs as soon as he was allowed to leave the table and flung himself on the bed.

He KNEW what he had seen. Leaning on the windowsill,

head under the curtains, he peered out into the rainy blackness. If only he'd been quick enough to take a picture.

Then, there it was again. But this time two lights and much lower down; then in the same way, they both shot upwards and shot off horizontally to the left.

The same way! thought Daniel – he was looking from the back of the house.

He didn't tell anyone about the second sighting; but he noted everything down in his special book. Then he looked on the internet: *What to do when you spot a UFO*

It was full of complicated instructions which he couldn't quite understand. So when he got to school the following day, he asked his really clever friend Kevin.

"Hmm," Kevin pondered to himself at first, pushing his oversized glasses further up the bridge of his nose, "you need to keep a record, then report it."

*

For the whole of the next week Daniel watched, sitting on his bedroom windowsill, and each day there was one more, all behaving in the same bizarre fashion.

Finally, at the end of the week, Daniel plucked up the courage to go outside into the back garden, pretending to his parents that he was helpfully taking out the rubbish.

He stood transfixed.

He was now watching seven lights all spinning in a perfect line, but this time they didn't just disappear; and, what's more, he could hear a set of low sounds, played over and over as if a radio was on with the volume turned down.

All at once the garden was flooded with an eerie green

light. His first instinct was to run straight back into the house where the rest of the family were relaxing, watching TV. Then just at the edge of the garden, he could see dark shapes, shifting and changing like shadows; but suddenly there were a series of bright flashes, for all the world as if someone was taking a picture.

After what seemed like ages, the shapes simply faded away and the light seemed to gradually weaken until the garden was completely dark again and there was nothing to see in the sky but stars.

Of course, he did finally share his encounter with his family who could sense he had experienced some kind of ordeal; but in reality they still thought he had been dreaming or sleepwalking. However, Dad helped him report it to the right authorities and after that he saw no more.

*

It was months later; Daniel had joined an online 'UFO sighting' group for kids and so he received lots of colourful brochures and goodies for his monthly subscription. One morning he saw an oddly-shaped triangular envelope on the mat. Thinking nothing of it, he stuffed it into his schoolbag and ran off, late as usual, just making the bus.

Fortunately, he managed to get a seat next to Kevin and started to undo this strange piece of post. Inside was a clear photograph of himself looking rather shocked, surrounded by the familiar things in his back garden. On the back was a simple message:

Thank you, we enjoyed our visit.

The Dancer

Lewis Dee had been to lots of schools. Not because his family had frequently moved house, but because he just couldn't behave.

"He really can't help himself," observed his last headteacher, "he needs careful handling, or maybe even special help."

So he was sent as a kind of last resort to St Mary's Primary, the largest school in the city with a 'good' reputation. A school which helped others to improve, where pupils behaved, and the teachers were exceptional – so said the school brochure.

Lewis' mum sighed as she ushered her errant son up the unfamiliar driveway. His younger brother's pushchair seemed heavier than usual and Lewis hung back, kicking at the gravel as he went.

"Now, don't start…" Mrs Dee warned weakly. Times were hard. No father on the scene, no family nearby, never enough money…

Lewis had become more and more difficult since his dad had disappeared, suddenly, without warning. She didn't really know how much longer she'd be able to cope.

Still, this seemed like a nice building and, well, she just wanted to get him out of her way for a few hours each day.

The new headteacher, Mr Morris, was kind, but all the same, the sort of teacher you didn't question, and he quickly summed up the situation, carefully choosing the class teacher with the most experience and calmest attitude. Mrs Smith had come across lots of children like this before.

"We'll try our best, Mrs Dee," Mr Morris spoke reassuringly, "but Lewis has got to try too."

She nodded and wiped her youngest son's nose.

"Can I go now?" – she was eager to avoid any more awkward questions.

So Lewis was taken along to his new Year 5 classroom where he behaved impeccably for the rest of the morning, only muttering when he was spoken to. Mrs Smith knew not to make too much of this, and chose Peter Grimes as a 'sensible friend' to take him out into the playground at playtime and lunchtime.

And that's where the trouble started. Peter introduced Lewis to the rest of the football gang, but the newcomer proceeded to kick the ball wildly into the bushes when it was evident that he couldn't play very well.

"Are you stupid or what?!" shouted Navir, captain of the school second team. "We'll get it confiscated now!"

Without hesitation, Lewis strode over and knocked Navir flying, so that he was covered in mud. Navir jumped to his feet, fists raised.

"Fight, fight, fight!" Everyone was gathered round in a flash.

Whistles blew, and both boys, now fully covered in mud, were hauled into the corridor outside the staffroom.

"Not a good start, Lewis," Mrs Smith spoke quietly at the end of playtime, "and Navir, I'm surprised at you."

This was the first of many incidents, and eventually, reluctantly, Mr Morris banned him from going outside at playtime or lunchtime.

"Just think why we have had to keep you in and what you are missing…" His words went unheeded and Lewis retreated once more into sulky silence. It was always the same…

*

Christmas was just around the corner, and Year 5 were responsible for the Key Stage 2 production. A script was produced: a reworking of *Aladdin*. The staff were very excited, all of them fond of drama, dancing and masses of glitz and glamour. Their enthusiasm was infectious and when they all met in the hall for *X Factor*-style auditions, the children and their teachers were beside themselves with anticipation.

Lewis found the whole process utterly tedious and predictably started to annoy people; kicking their shoes as he sat beside them, flicking pieces of paper into their hair; nothing major, but he soon found himself sitting on his own next to the teachers.

"Where I can see you!" Mrs Smith said with a sigh.

All speaking parts cast, now it was time to sort out groups of dancers.

"Everybody dances!" Mrs Smith beamed at them all. So everybody had to get up and go through a routine. Lewis stood awkwardly, not moving; he'd never danced and didn't intend to start now.

*

Eventually, playtime came and Lewis had to stand and watch all the others go out. However, four of the boys met in the hall to try out for some special dancing parts. They were trying to do backflips and none of them were managing it. Mrs Smith looked at her watch.

"Right, hold on, boys; I'm going to get a coffee, just sit and wait a minute."

She left, motioning to Lewis to turn around outside the hall window.

"What are you looking at?" Rahul spotted Lewis staring through the glass. He personally found him quite interesting and he had never been upset by him; so he popped his head round the door. "You any good at backflips? Because we're rubbish!"

Lewis crept into the hall. The others looked at him warily. He stood, trying to look cool, hands in pockets.

"Yep, I can do that!"

"Go on then!" Tom was dubious.

Lewis ran to the back of the hall and launched himself full pelt towards the stage, then leapt up and turned over twice, before landing steadily on his feet without, it seemed, even getting out of breath.

"Whoah!" All the boys were impressed, and at that moment, Mrs Smith walked back into the room, immediately glowering at Lewis.

"You are supposed to be outside, young man!"

"But, Miss," interrupted Rahul, "you should see him do a backflip!"

"Yes, Miss, let him show you!" Tom interjected generously.

"Well now, Lewis," Mrs Smith wisely took a close look

at Lewis, who had an uncharacteristic spark of interest in his eye. "Let's see it then."

Lewis walked slowly to the back of the hall and repeated his astonishing move, somersaulting even higher this time. The other boys spontaneously applauded.

Mrs Smith smiled. "And what else can you do, Lewis?"

Lively upbeat music was selected and Mrs Smith led them all through a few basic street moves, Lewis included. He moved uncertainly at first, but soon let the music flow through him and easily outshone the rest of the group.

The bell signalling the end of playtime rang and the boys crowded round Lewis excitedly.

"Hey, you're really good, man…"

"Is he going to be in it, Miss?" All their voices clamoured excitedly at once.

Mrs Smith drew Lewis aside. "Well, it's up to you, Lewis. Would you like to join us?"

He looked uncertain. No one had asked him to be in anything before.

"Of course, that depends on your behaviour…" Mrs Smith moved on quickly, "but I'm sure that will be fine, won't it?!"

Lewis looked slightly dubious.

"Don't you worry, Miss. We'll make sure of that!" Rahul winked at the others.

And they were true to their word. At playtime, whenever Lewis looked as if he was going to get into an argument, one of the dance group would march him firmly away from the situation. Whenever he started getting fidgety in assembly, he would find four other sets of eyes staring at him until he stopped. Whenever they were due to rehearse, he would be scooped up by them all and consequently made all the meetings on time.

*

The night of the performance came around quickly. The whole of Year 5 were simply bursting with excitement. The children were due back at school at 6pm for 'make-up and costumes'.

Lewis' mum was reluctant to come. He had never been in a school play before and she was sure he would misbehave and show her up once more. It was difficult getting his younger brother ready to go because he was really tired and fractious.

"Are you sure you want to be in it?" his mum asked a little grumpily. "Normally you're not bothered!"

"Well, I *am* this time. Come *on*, Cameron!"

Eventually, he persuaded his brother to get into the pushchair and they made their way along the gleaming wet pavements, his mum trying hard to keep up with her eldest son, who for once seemed to be actually keen on going to school.

He left them both at the door and dashed off to his classroom; the rest of the boys were already there.

"Thank goodness for that!" Rahul grabbed hold of his arm. "Thought you weren't coming, get your costume on!"

Mrs Smith had fitted them out in really smart black outfits complete with 'beanie' hats. It was like a team strip. She looked at them proudly:

"I can't wait to see your scene, boys. Spread out, heads up and don't forget to smile!"

Lewis felt slightly sick. What if he fell over? What if everyone laughed?

But then it all started and he found himself standing in the 'wings', waiting to go on next to Rahul.

"Go on then, mate; show 'em what you're made of!"

And there he was on stage, blinking in the bright lights. The familiar music started and he could just make out Mrs Smith standing at the back holding up a big sign which read:

Smile and enjoy it!

The applause was thunderous when Lewis performed his double backflip; as he landed he caught sight of his mum's face. She had never looked so happy.

Mr Morris gave him a special mention in his speech at the end and as Lewis walked out of school, his mum's arm around his shoulders, a young Year 3 boy pointed at him.

"That's Lewis Dee – the brilliant dancer!"

Lewis grinned to himself. Not 'the troublemaker' or 'the naughty boy', just 'the brilliant dancer'. It sounded good.

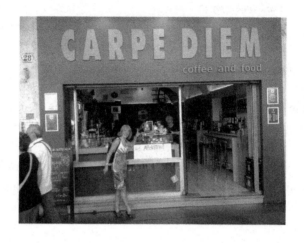

Melody has taught in Primary schools for nearly 40 years
and continues to share her enthusiasm with teachers as
part of their continued professional development mainly
in P.E. and dance. Since the publication of her first book
"Extraordinary Shorts", she enjoys delivering writing
workshops and events for staff and children. She is also
a governor at Eastern Green Junior School in Coventry
where she lives with her husband Alan. She is very much
involved with the local community that celebrates the rich
culture of the city as part of the Godiva Sisters Association.

She passionately believes in the value of the arts and
creative projects in schools and again hopes this book will
inspire children to create imaginative works of their own.

Beth Blake has drawn since childhood, fascinated by imaginary worlds of Narnia and The Borrowers and would spend many an hour pouring over the captivating illustrations accompanying the text.

Her creative journey has taken her from A level Art to Dewsbury School of Art, then on to a BA Hons degree from Manchester Metropolitan University.

Beth works as a freelance artist and illustrator from her home studio in Coventry where she lives with her husband, two children and animals who are all at the heart of the inspiration for her work.